The Mystery
of the
Treasure Map

Story by Andrew Richardson   Illustrations by Patrick Girouard

RSVP

RAINTREE
STECK-VAUGHN
P U B L I S H E R S

The Steck-Vaughn Company

Austin, Texas

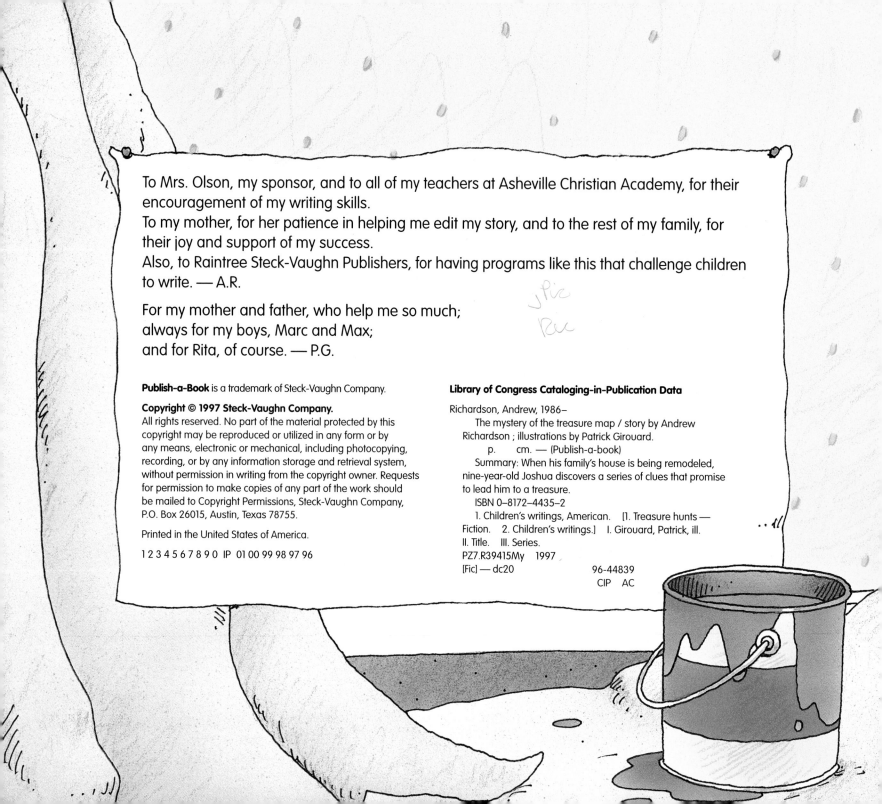

To Mrs. Olson, my sponsor, and to all of my teachers at Asheville Christian Academy, for their encouragement of my writing skills.
To my mother, for her patience in helping me edit my story, and to the rest of my family, for their joy and support of my success.
Also, to Raintree Steck-Vaughn Publishers, for having programs like this that challenge children to write. — A.R.

For my mother and father, who help me so much;
always for my boys, Marc and Max;
and for Rita, of course. — P.G.

Publish-a-Book is a trademark of Steck-Vaughn Company.

Copyright © 1997 Steck-Vaughn Company.

Printed in the United States of America.

1 2 3 4 5 6 7 8 9 0 IP 01 00 99 98 97 96

Library of Congress Cataloging-in-Publication Data

Richardson, Andrew, 1986–
    The mystery of the treasure map / story by Andrew Richardson ; illustrations by Patrick Girouard.
        p.   cm. — (Publish-a-book)
    Summary: When his family's house is being remodeled, nine-year-old Joshua discovers a series of clues that promise to lead him to a treasure.
    ISBN 0–8172–4435–2
    1. Children's writings, American.   [1. Treasure hunts —
Fiction.   2. Children's writings.]   I. Girouard, Patrick, ill.
II. Title.   III. Series.
PZ7.R39415My   1997
[Fic] — dc20   96-44839
                                      CIP   AC

The Turner family was having some repairs done on their house. Nine-year-old Joshua was *very* bored. He was bugging the workers who were taking out the windows in the family room. A piece of crumpled paper fell to the floor as they took out the third window.

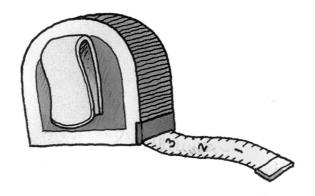

Jack, one of the workers, reached down and handed the paper to Joshua. "Here, son. This will keep you busy for a while. It looks like a treasure map. See if you can solve the mystery and find the treasure."

BASEBALL FACTS

REDS

Joshua ran up to his bedroom. He uncrumpled the paper. It was wrinkled and faded, but he could still read it. The map looked as if it had been written by a boy close to his age. It was dated 1973. The directions at the top of the page said, "Solve the mystery and the treasure is yours!"

Joshua was excited. He followed the map to the basement wall. Peering into a crack, he saw a folded sheet of paper. He ran to get needlenose pliers from one of the workers. Hurrying back to the crack, he stuck the pliers in and pulled the paper out. It was another map.

This map led him to a light fixture in the upstairs guest bedroom. He found Bob, one of the workers, and talked him into taking down the light fixture. Sure enough, there above the fixture was another piece of paper.

14

"Now leave me alone, son. Here's a flashlight. Go find the next clue by yourself. I need to get my work done," said Bob.

Joshua read the map. It led him to the kitchen. Jack and Mike were just taking down the cabinets that were marked on his map.

Joshua yelled, "Stop! My next clue should be in those cabinets!"

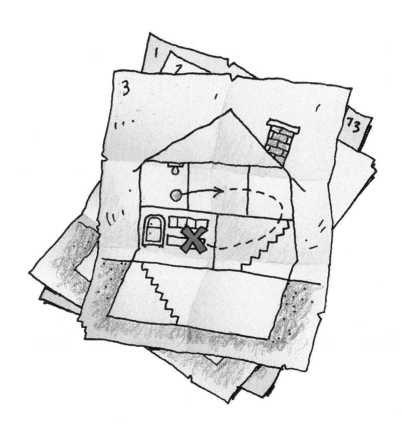

"Sorry, son," said Mike. "We have to get our work done."

Just then, Joshua spied something in the hole where the cabinets had been. Reaching for it, he pulled out another map.

This map led him to an old picture that had been in the house even before his family had moved there. Joshua carefully took the picture down. Removing the back, he saw a baseball card. He took it out and ran downstairs to show Jack.

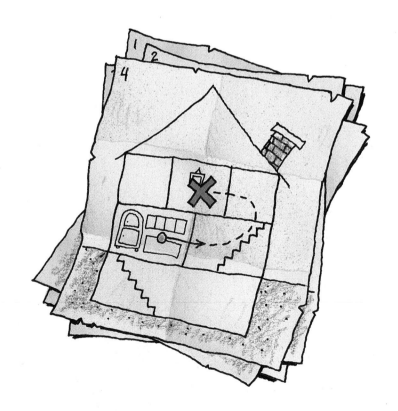

Jack looked up from his work and rolled his eyes at Joshua. "What now, kid?"

Joshua held out the card. "I think I found the treasure," he said.

Walking over to Jack, Bob couldn't believe his eyes. He took the card from Joshua and said, "Son, this is a Johnny Bench rookie card from 1968. This card is worth some money."

Rolling his eyes again, Jack said, "Can you beat that? The kid really did find a treasure."

Andrew William Richardson, author of **The Mystery of the Treasure Map**, was born on June 26, 1986, in Seymour, Indiana, to Michael and Linda Richardson. He moved with his family to Asheville, North Carolina, in 1988. Andrew is the oldest of four children. His brother and sisters, from oldest to youngest, are Caroline (Kiki), Sarah, and Philip. Andrew attends Asheville Christian Academy, where he plays clarinet in the school orchestra. His other interests include playing the piano, coin collecting, writing, reading, assembling models, and using the computer. Andrew also enjoys giving piano lessons and participating in Cub Scouts.

Andrew wrote about a treasure map because he likes to set up treasure hunts for his brother and sisters at home. At school, he and his friends bury things at recess, then see how long the "treasures" can stay buried before somebody else finds them. Andrew hopes someday to find an old treasure map like the one Joshua found in the story.

The ten honorable-mention winners in the **1996 Raintree/Steck-Vaughn Young Publish-a-Book™ Contest** were Aaron White, North Ridge Magnet School, Moreno Valley, California; Brent D. Kish, Edgewood Campus School, Madison, Wisconsin; Sarah E. Withrow, Edison Elementary School, South Charleston, West Virginia; Molly S. Mellinger, Riverfield School, Fairfield, Connecticut; Alexis Lee Jackson, Lincoln Elementary School, Norman, Oklahoma; Jessica C. Prater, Trimble Elementary School, Trimble, Tennessee; Brittany Brown, Early Elementary School, Early, Texas; Thomas E. Eng, Norwood Creek School, San Jose, California; Sarah Stephens, Gwynedd Square Elementary School, Lansdale, Pennsylvania; Jason M. Collins, Sallie Zetterower Elementary School, Statesboro, Georgia.

Patrick Girouard has two cool sons, has played tuba for six years (not constantly), collects toy cameras, has a secret name, and has worked in an ice factory. He has been a dog groomer, bus driver, landscaper, cook, graphic artist, and medical test subject. He is left-handed on paper but right-handed on a chalkboard and loves to draw pictures. He has a bird named Jane, two brothers, one sister, two stepbrothers, two stepsisters, and one half sister. He would like to thank Mr. Tim Schlax of Mundelein, Illinois, for his help in finding a 1968 Johnny Bench rookie card.